OLIVIA
Builds a Snowlady

adapted by Farrah McDoogle
based on the screenplay written by Gabe Pulliam
illustrated by Guy Wolek

Simon Spotlight
New York   London   Toronto   Sydney

Based on the TV series *OLIVIA*™ as seen on Nickelodeon™

SIMON SPOTLIGHT
An imprint of Simon & Schuster Children's Publishing Division
1230 Avenue of the Americas, New York, New York 10020
For information about special discounts for bulk purchases, please contact
Simon & Schuster Special Sales at 1-866-506-1949 or business@simonandschuster.com.
Manufactured in the United States of America 0911 LAK
First Edition
1 2 3 4 5 6 7 8 9 10
ISBN 978-1-4424-3286-4

"Something very special is happening this weekend!" Mrs. H. said. "Does anybody know what it is?"

Harold raised his hand. "My mom is taking me to get long underwear?"

"No, not that," said Mrs. H. as the class giggled.

Olivia raised her hand. "I know," she said, "It's the Maywood Winter Festival!"

"That's right!" replied Mrs. H. "And what or, should I say, *who* is the most important part of the winter festival?"

"THE SNOWMAN!" the class answered all together.

Every year someone new is put in charge of building the snowman for the winter festival. It is a very special honor.

"This year our class will be in charge of the snowman!" Mrs. H. announced. "What kind of snowman should we make?"

There were so many ideas!

"A snow clown!" suggested Francine.

"Twin snowmen!" suggested Otto and Oscar.

"A snowman who is perfect and small—just like me!" suggested Daisy.

Olivia had an idea. "I wonder . . . ," she thought. "How about . . . a snow*lady*? The biggest snowlady the town has ever seen!" said Olivia. Everyone cheered. What a great idea!

The next day Olivia met up with Francine and Harold to build the snowlady.

"Thanks for helping," Olivia said to her friends.

"No problem," said Francine. "But what is *that*?" she asked, pointing to a loud machine that Ian and Father were tinkering with.

"Oh, that's my mom's cotton-candy machine," Olivia explained. "Ian wants to sell cotton candy at the festival."

"Now let's get down to business," Olivia continued. She rolled out a blueprint for Harold and Francine to see. "Here's the plan. . . ."

Olivia, Francine, and Harold got to work.
Harold went to find things to make the snowlady's face.

Olivia and Francine rolled some snowballs. The snowballs got bigger and bigger . . . until they were giant-size!

"Wow, these snowballs are huge," said Francine. "There's no way we can lift another snowball all the way up there!"
"Who said anything about lifting it?" replied Olivia. "We'll use a ramp!"

"Now prepare to launch!" Olivia called to Francine after they had constructed their ramp. Just as Olivia launched the snowball, Harold showed up, holding a big carrot and lumps of coal.
"Look out!" called Olivia and Francine. But it was too late.

Luckily for Harold, the giant snowball just rolled right over him. And as it rolled over him, it picked up the carrot and lumps of coal before landing softly on top of the other two snowballs.

"Wow, she's as big as a dinosaur!" said Ian.
"The snowlady is beautiful," added Father.
"Building a snowlady is hard work. Great job, everyone," Olivia said.

The next day was the day of the festival. Olivia woke up feeling very excited.

"Look alive, everybody! Grab your mittens and scarves! We have to get to the festival!" said Olivia as she rushed into the kitchen.

Then Olivia looked out the window and saw that it was a very sunny day outside. Very sunny indeed.
"Uh-oh," said Olivia.

Later, at the festival grounds, Olivia looked around for the beautiful snowlady. At first she couldn't find her . . . and then she spotted her.

"What happened to the snowlady?" asked Harold.

"She melted," said Olivia.

"Oh, no!" cried Francine.

"What will we do?" asked Harold.

In the distance Olivia's father fired up the cotton-candy machine, and it gave Olivia a wonderful idea.

"Harold, Francine, we're building a bigger, better snowlady!" she said excitedly.

"But the snow is too slushy!" Francine pointed out.

"Who needs snow?" Olivia exclaimed. "We have something better!"

"The thing about cotton candy," Olivia explained to her friends, "is that you have to twirl it!"

Olivia twirled and twirled.
Francine twirled and twirled.

Harold twirled . . . and got dizzy.
So Ian helped out and twirled.

"All right, twirlers, that should do it!" Olivia called. Then she whistled and moments later, Perry appeared with Olivia's trunk on a sled. "And now to put it all together!" Olivia told her friends.
Soon the cotton-candy snowlady had a face made of rubber-ball eyes and a watermelon mouth. A tinfoil tiara sat on top of her head. She towered over the crowd that had gathered.

"Ladies and gentlemen, I present to you the world's biggest and *pinkest* snowlady!" Olivia exclaimed.

Everyone oohed and aahed.

"This is the most magnificent snowlady I have ever seen!" said Mrs. H.

"And the tastiest," added Harold.

"Let the winter festival begin!" cried Olivia.

Later that night, it was time for bed.

"Olivia, that was the best winter festival ever, thanks to you and your snowlady," said Olivia's mother.

"Thanks, Mom," said Olivia. "I think I'll make a cotton-candy igloo next! Or maybe a cotton-candy cruise ship . . ."

"That sounds wonderful," replied Mother. "I can't wait for next year's festival. Good night, Olivia."